HIG-JUV

Ladybird

This Little Story

belongs to

_____

Published by Ladybird Books Ltd
80 Strand London WC2R 0RL
A Penguin Company
5 7 9 10 8 6
© LADYBIRD BOOKS LTD MCMXCVIII

Printed in Italy

Helpful
Little
Mechanic

by Margaret Eustace

illustrated by Tony Kenyon

"Right, lads," said the Chief Mechanic, wiping his greasy hands on his greasy overalls. "Mr Granville Grenville (Senior) has just phoned to say he has a Most Important Meeting this afternoon, and his big, red, shiny car won't start.

"As you know," he went on, "he is a Very Important Person, and it's up to us to save the day!"

"Right," said the Second Mechanic. "I'll get the tools ready."

And he opened out the big, blue tool box, full of big spanners, little spanners, big screwdrivers, little screwdrivers and spare packets of bubble gum.

"Right," said the Third Mechanic. "I'll open the big doors."

And he heaved on the rusty handles until the big doors rolled back on their rusty little wheels.

"Excuse me, please…" said the Helpful Little Mechanic.

"Not now!" they all said. "This is a job for the experts. You just go and make us all a drink." And so he did.

The Very Important Person's car
arrived on the back of the big
breakdown truck.

"Now, then," said the Chief
Mechanic, sipping his tea.
"We'll soon have this sorted."

They lifted the bonnet of
Mr Granville Grenville's car and
then they all peered inside.

"Well, boys?" said the Chief
Mechanic. "What do you think?"

"No worries!" said the Second Mechanic, sliding the dipstick down into the engine as far as he could reach.

"Oil looks all right but I'll just top it up, to be on the safe side."

So the Second Mechanic fetched the oily oil can and topped up the oil – GLOOP! GLOOP! GLOOP! Then he wiped the dipstick on the side of his trousers!

Your mum will be after you.

"Easy-peasy!" said the Third Mechanic, taking off the radiator cap and admiring his own reflection in the water. "Water looks all right but I'll just top it up, to be on the safe side."

So the Third Mechanic fetched the battered watering can and topped up the radiator – SHLOOSH! SHLOOSH! SHLOOSH! – until it overflowed and got his socks all wet.

My toes are soaked!

"Excuse me, please…" said the Helpful Little Mechanic.

"Not now!" they all said. "This job needs brains. You just go and make us all another drink." And so he did.

"Should be fine now," said the Chief Mechanic, sipping his next cup of tea. "Start her up!"

The Second Mechanic got in and turned the key.

Whirr – whirr – whirr went the engine, but it wouldn't start.

"Oh dear," said the Chief Mechanic, scratching his head.

"Excuse me, please..." said the Helpful Little Mechanic.

"Not now!" they all said. "Can't you see we've got a problem here? You just go and make us all another drink." And so he did.

"Let's jack the car up, boys," said the Chief Mechanic, sipping his tea. They took it in turns to slide underneath for a better look.

The Chief Mechanic took out lots of bits with his big spanners. The Second Mechanic laid them out on the work bench. The Third Mechanic polished them all up...

And then they put them all back again.

Clean as a whistle.

"Should be fine now!" said the
Chief Mechanic. "Start her up!"

The Third Mechanic climbed in and
turned the key.

Whirr–*whirr*–*whirr* went the engine,
but it still wouldn't start.

"This is more serious than I thought," said the Chief Mechanic. "I'll go and look for the instruction book."

"Perhaps Mr Granville Grenville (Senior) could catch the bus," said the Second Mechanic.

"He could borrow my bike," said the Third Mechanic, "as long as he's careful with it!"

If in doubt read the instructions.

"Excuse me, please…" said the Helpful Little Mechanic.

"Not now!" they all said. "We have to put our heads together. You just go and make us all another drink." And so he did.

They all sat down in the office, stirring their tea and looking thoughtful.

"Hmmm," said the Chief Mechanic. "After all that tea – I just need to pop out for a moment."

"And me!" said the Second Mechanic.

"And me!" said the Third Mechanic.

Could you hurry up please!

While they were gone, the Helpful
Little Mechanic walked back
into the garage and looked at
Mr Granville Grenville's big, red,
shiny car. He fetched a petrol can
and carefully filled the petrol tank.
Then he slipped behind the wheel,
held his breath and turned the key.

whirr-whirr-whirr

Whirr – whirr – whirr went the engine.

Then *tick-a-tick-a-tick*.

And then *brrmm – brrmm – brrmmm!*

"What's that I hear?" cried the Chief Mechanic, running back in.

"Success at last!" yelled the Second Mechanic.

"Three cheers for us!" whooped the Third Mechanic, doing cartwheels across the oily floor.

"Here comes the Very Important Person," said the Helpful Little Mechanic proudly.

"I knew I could rely on you!" beamed Mr Granville Grenville (Senior). "Now I'm off to visit my mum at the seaside. I know how busy you all must be, so I'll just take the Little Mechanic with me for a treat!"

"Thank you," smiled the Helpful Little Mechanic. "Shall I just make another drink before I go?"

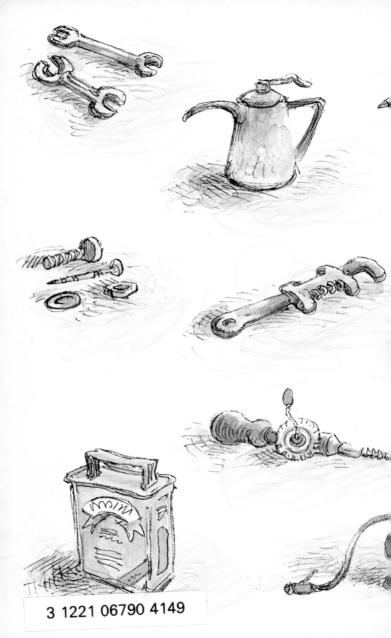